"I DON'T LIKE CHOOSE YOUR OWN ADVENTURE® BOOKS. I *LOVE* THEM!" says Jessica Gordon, age ten. And now, kids between the ages of six and nine can choose their own adventures too. Here's what kids have to say about the Skylark Choose Your Own Adventure® books.

"These are my favorite books because you can pick whatever choice you want— and the story is all about you."

—**Katy Alson,** *age 8*

"I love finding out how my story will end."

—**Joss Williams,** *age 9*

"I like all the illustrations!"

—**Savitri Brightfield,** *age 7*

"A six-year-old friend and I have lots of fun making the decisions together!"

—**Peggy Marcus** *(adult)*

Bantam Skylark Books in the Choose Your Own Adventure®
    Series
Ask your bookseller for the books you have missed

THE GREAT EASTER BUNNY ADVENTURE

EDWARD PACKARD

ILLUSTRATED BY VINCENT BELL

A Packard/Montgomery Book

A BANTAM SKYLARK BOOK®

TORONTO · NEW YORK · LONDON · SYDNEY · AUCKLAND

RL 2, 007-009

THE GREAT EASTER BUNNY ADVENTURE
A Bantam Skylark Book / April 1987

*CHOOSE YOUR OWN ADVENTURE® is a registered
trademark of Bantam Books, Inc.*

Original conception of Edward Packard.

*Skylark Books is a registered trademark of
Bantam Books, Inc.
Registered in U.S. Patent and Trademark Office
and elsewhere.*

MAY 9 1988

ISBN 0-553-15492-3

Published simultaneously in the United States and Canada

---

*Bantam Books are published by Bantam Books, Inc. Its trade-
mark, consisting of the words "Bantam Books" and the por-
trayal of a rooster, is registered in U.S. Patent and Trademark
Office and in other countries. Marca Registrada. Bantam
Books, Inc., 666 Fifth Avenue, New York, New York 10103.*

PRINTED IN THE UNITED STATES OF AMERICA

CW   0 9 8 7 6 5 4 3 2 1

THE GREAT EASTER BUNNY ADVENTURE

READ THIS FIRST!!!

Most books are about other people.

This book is about you, and what happens to you on a very special Easter morning.

Do not read this book from the first page through to the last page. Instead, start at page one and read until you come to your first choice. Decide what you want to do. Then turn to the page shown and see what happens.

When you come to the end of a story, go back and try another choice. Every choice leads to a new adventure.

Are you ready to meet the Easter bunny? Then turn to page one . . . and good luck!

It's Easter morning, and you've woken up **1** very early. It's just beginning to get light outside. You peer out the window. In the faint light you can barely see the soft brown shape in your backyard. It's a rabbit!

That must be the Easter bunny, you think. You've always wondered why people talk about the Easter bunny instead of the Easter *bear* or the Easter *mouse*. Maybe there's something special about the Easter bunny, something magical. Maybe this Easter you can find out. You quickly get dressed and head outdoors.

You cross the lawn and walk slowly toward the bunny. "Good bunny," you say softly. "Nice bunny." Now you're right next to it, and it still hasn't moved. Slowly you move your hand over the bunny and gently pat his back. Maybe he'd like some lettuce; it sure would surprise your family to see the Easter bunny in the house!

Turn to page 2.

2 You pick up the bunny gently but firmly so he won't hop out of your arms. His light brown hair is soft as silk. His whole body is quivering.

Holding the bunny in one arm, you get some lettuce from the fridge, then a bowl, and head for your bedroom. You close the door behind you and set the bunny on the floor and the bowl of lettuce next to him. "Good bunny," you say, stroking his back.

The bunny sits quietly, still quivering a little. He probably won't eat the lettuce till he feels more at home, you think. Then you realize you're feeling sleepy—you don't usually wake up this early.

"Why don't you rest awhile, bunny," you say, "and I will too."

You climb into bed, pull up the covers, and drift dreamily back to sleep.

Turn to page 10.

The Indian leads you along a path through the forest. The first rays of sunlight cast a pink glow on the trees. A red-billed woodpecker skims over your head. The Indian places her hand against the rough, wet bark of a tulip tree. You do the same. It feels good to your touch.

"This tree is talking to us," she says.

You reach a brook running through the forest. You listen to it gurgling. You smell the wet, green grass and chives growing along the water's edge.

"This brook is talking to you," the Indian says.

She reaches into the water and picks up a beautiful stone, bone white and shaped like a perfect egg. She holds it out to you. As you take it in your hand, you suddenly find yourself back in your own bed!

You open your hand and the egg-shaped stone falls on the bedspread.

"Happy Easter!" your mom calls from outside your door.

The End

6 You walk toward the farmhouse in the distance. Suddenly a girl comes out. "Happy Easter!" she calls. "I've never seen you around. My name's Caroline. Where did you tie up your horse?"

"Happy Easter!" you call back, but you hardly hear your own voice. You're trying to figure things out.

Caroline's mother appears at the door and invites you in to join the family for breakfast. When you tell your story, her eyes open wide.

"I'm afraid this child fell off a horse," she says to her husband. "You'd better ride to town and fetch Doc Mathers."

When you hear this, you decide to try to find your way home. You run out the door, across the pasture and into the woods, back to the forking path.

If you take the right-hand fork toward where your house used to be, turn to page 13.

If you take the left-hand fork where the bunny went, turn to page 50.

"What was it like where I lived before the **9** Indians came?" you ask the bunny.

Suddenly you're blinking your eyes—it's so bright. And cold! The whole world has changed again—this time in a way that's even harder to believe. You're standing on a thick crust of snow. Everywhere you look are fields of ice and snow with huge slabs of blue-white ice sticking up here and there. There are no trees or houses—no signs of life at all. You're shivering. Your ears and nose tingle. You might as well be at the North Pole!

The bunny is sitting in the snow. "We're in the Ice Age now," he says.

"Everything has been killed by the ice!" you say.

"No, the land is only sleeping," the bunny replies. "Watch!"

Turn to page 30.

10   When you wake up, the bunny is sitting near the door. His head is tilted and one eye is fixed on you. There's something strange about the way he's looking at you. . . . He wants to go outside, and he wants you to follow him!

Out on the lawn you rub your eyes in disbelief. The houses you could see from your backyard are gone! And when you look around, you see your own house is gone too. In its place is a path leading into the woods. This is terrible! How could things have changed so?

Ahead of you the path forks. The bunny is hopping into the woods along the right fork. The left-hand fork leads into a pasture where some cows are grazing. Beyond them is a big red barn and a farmhouse—yet you're certain there was no farm near your house!

*If you head for the farmhouse,
turn to page 6.*

*If you keep following the bunny,
turn to page 27.*

You take the right-hand fork. Soon, ahead of you through the woods, you see a house. Thank goodness—it's yours!

You run inside. No one's up yet, so you go back to your bedroom and crawl under the covers.

"What just happened?" you ask yourself. There's only one explanation: The Easter bunny showed you your neighborhood as it was about a hundred years ago!

The End

14   The wind blows against your face. Sleet stings your cheeks. Your feet feel like lead weights as you drag them through the snow. At last you reach an icy ridge and topple over the edge—into a meadow filled with flowers!

You hold your cold hands to the warm spring sun. Thank goodness, you made it out of the Ice Age!

"Am I back in my own time?" you ask the bunny.

"Far from it," he replies. "We're in the future. This is where your house was a million years ago!"

In the distance past the meadow is a sparkling lake; beyond it, snowcapped mountains. You're sorry that someday your house will be gone. Yet you're glad that in the future your backyard will be filled with beautiful flowers.

That's why you're smiling when you wake up minutes later, snug in your own bed on Easter morning!

The End

You run to keep up with the bunny. With each step the forest is changing. Suddenly there are lots more birch trees in the woods. *Whoosh!* An arrow whistles by your ear. You stop short, then turn and stare as three men with black hair and copper-hued skin run toward you. They're Indians, and they are as surprised to see you as you are to see them. They talk excitedly. You can't understand their language, but it sounds as if the one who shot the arrow thought you were a deer.

Go on to the next page.

18   The Indians lead you through the woods. One of them speaks a little English. He tells you they are taking you back to their camp. You're curious to see an Indian camp, but you're also a little afraid of what might happen there.

Suddenly you see the bunny, watching you from a clump of laurel.

If you run toward the bunny, turn to page 22.

If you stay with the Indians, turn to page 25.

Slowly you open your eyes. You're back in **19** bed! It must have all been a dream, except the bunny is still there beside you. At least you weren't dreaming about that!

Later in the morning you call some neighbors, but you can't find anyone who lost a bunny. You take him out on the lawn again. The bunny looks at you, his nose quivering, then hops away through the brush.

You wonder what would happen if you followed him. Maybe what you dreamed would really happen! That's a scary thought because this time you wouldn't wake up from it back in your bed. This time you might never get home again.

Despite these thoughts, you run after the bunny. But you've waited too long. No matter where you look, you can't find him. That's just as well, you think—he has his world and I have mine.

The End

The bunny races across the mossy bank
and darts in among a clump of ferns. As you
run after him, the ferns begin to shrink. The
ground becomes soft and squishy. The air
smells of smoke. It comes from a nearby vol-
cano. Smoke and fire belch from its cone.

The bunny stops; he sits quivering. You
wonder if he's as frightened as you.

"It's hard to breathe here," you say. "Were
the dinosaurs killed by volcanos?"

The bunny shakes his head. "You don't
understand," he says. "We've gone even farther back in time. The first dinosaur hasn't
been born yet!"

The bunny hops along the ground. The
grass, flowers, woods, and plants have disappeared. The world around you now is only
rock and clay and pools of water.

"The world looks dead," you say.

"No," the bunny replies. "It's just being
born—not here, but in the oceans—that's
where life on earth began."

Turn to page 28.

22   As you run toward the bunny, the Indians start after you. But you dart in among the laurel and then out of it into a completely different scene! The land around you is covered with tundra, strange-looking short grass. Huge rocks stick up from the ground here and there. From the ridge where you're standing you can see at least a dozen ponds and lakes. In the hollows are deep banks of snow. A herd of animals is grazing in the distance—they're caribou!

The bunny sits only a few feet away. You hadn't noticed him because he's the same color as the tundra. He talked before, you think; maybe he'll talk again. "Please," you ask, "where are we now?"

"We're still in the same place," the bunny says, his nose twitching. "But we're fifteen thousand years in the past!"

Turn to page 36.

You find that the Indians live in long, flat-roofed, log houses covered with animal hides and bark. In the center of the village, meat is cooking over an open fire. Animal skins have been hung out to dry. Children are playing a game with acorns. They stop and stare at you.

Go on to the next page.

26   An Indian woman walks toward you. She offers you a bowl of food and a stick flattened at one end for use as a spoon. In the bowl is a mixture of blueberries and something that tastes like celery.

"How did you get here?" the Indian asks.

"I was looking for the Easter bunny."

"Were you looking for the bunny because you'd like to learn what he knows?"

"Yes," you answer.

"Then you must listen to the Earth," the Indian tells you. "Come with me, and you shall see."

Turn to page 5.

The bunny hops along a path through the **27** woods. You're able to keep up with him for a while, but you're getting tired.

"Stop!" you call. "Where are you going?"

You don't expect the bunny to answer. You only yell because you want him to wait. But the bunny calls back, "I'm going to where we came from."

"Where did we come from?" you ask.

"All life began in the sea," the bunny replies.

"But we can't go back there now," you protest.

The bunny stops short and sits very still for a moment, thinking about what you said. "You're right," he says. "I'd better take you back to your own time. Or would you rather go beyond your own time, into the future?"

If you want to go back to your own time, turn to page 40.

If you want to go into the future, turn to page 37.

28   Suddenly you feel faint. You can't seem to catch your breath. The bunny looks sick too. He sits on his haunches, panting for breath.

"What's happened?" you gasp.

"There's hardly . . . any oxygen . . . in the air here," the bunny says between breaths.

"Why?"

"Because . . . that's the way . . . the world was. We're two billion years in the past!"

You try to answer, but you can barely get enough air to breathe.

Turn to page 19.

30 The white snow swirls before your eyes; a breeze fans your face. Suddenly, as if you are watching a movie in fast forward, the whiteness turns to brown and then to green. Herds of bison and woolly mammoths lumber across the plain. Trees appear. They grow taller around you. Men chop them down with axes. Logs and branches are hauled away. Grass and flowers spring up. Cows wander across the new meadows. A barn appears; around it, acres of corn and pasture land. Then the farm grows smaller. Where cows and horses grazed, houses suddenly appear. One of them looks familiar! It's your house! You're only a few steps from home!

No one else in the family is up yet, but you've already learned what the Easter bunny knows: that winter follows autumn, but spring follows winter; that the earth itself lives and dies and is reborn again.

The End

Suddenly you know that you're millions and millions of years in the past. There's no doubt of it—because of the warm, moist landscape around you, the tall ferns and strange-looking fir trees, and most of all because of the enormous dinosaur—an allosaurus—grazing only a few hundred feet away!

Eeeks! You must be at least sixty-five million years in the past, and that dinosaur may be standing right where your house will be! As a matter of fact, it's about the same size as your house.

You're not in danger for the moment, the allosaurus eats only plants. And there's the Easter bunny, scampering across the bank of thick, spongy moss. Then you see an egg big as a football nestled in a hollow.

Some Easter egg! If only you could bring it home!

If you run after the bunny, turn to page 21.

If you stop to pick up the egg, turn to page 39.

34   You see three hunters armed with muskets.

"Whoa, where did you come from?" says one. "You must be lost. It's lucky you met us instead of a wolf."

They take you to their village. One of them invites you to his log house. His wife and children are waiting. You're chilled to the bone, and glad when they give you a bowl of hot corn soup.

"Is today Easter?" you ask.

"No. Easter was three days ago," says one child.

This puzzles you until you remember that Easter falls on a different date each year.

"What year is this?" you ask.

"Why, it's 1687." The hunter's wife touches your forehead. "I think you have a fever; you'd better go straight to bed."

"We found a bunny," says another child. She runs from the room and returns with the bunny in her arms.

Turn to page 43.

Fifteen thousand years! You're getting even farther away from your own time! But by now you're so used to having things mixed up that you're not quite as scared as you were, at least until you look around. Several men with spears are hiding behind a big rock!

So this is what it was like fifteen thousand years ago! Bows and arrows have not yet been invented. You wonder what it was like even farther back in time.

As if he understands your thoughts, the bunny says, "Would you like to see what it was like where you live even farther in the past—before the first Indians came? Or would you rather go back millions and millions of years?"

If you would like to see how your neighborhood looked before the first Indians came, turn to page 9.

If you would like to go back millions and millions of years before that, turn to page 33.

"Let's go even farther into the future," you
say.

"Come then," says the bunny. "We've no time to lose."

Suddenly all the trees have disappeared, and there are no landmarks to guide you. What's more, it's beginning to snow! Indeed, you're walking on a crust of ice and snow, and there's nothing else in sight!

Turn to page 44.

You can barely lift the egg. There must be a **39** baby dinosaur inside! If only you could get it back home. It would be the greatest Easter egg of all time.

ARREHH-HRAA! Two huge, leathery legs are moving toward you! Looking up, you see the enormous frame of tyrannosaurus rex. Its open jaws are lined with spikes. Its mouth is three times as long as you are tall!

ARRGHHH! It lunges toward you. You dive into a hollow. The earth trembles as the tyrannosaurus charges by. Only then do you realize it was chasing the allosaurus—you were too small for it to notice!

The bunny calls from the ridge above you. "Hurry or you'll never reach home."

You glance at the egg. You can't carry it and keep up with the bunny.

Turn to page 46.

"This is too weird," you say. "I'd like to go back to my own time."

"Then stay close to me," says the bunny as he bounds through the woods.

Running behind him, you struggle to keep up. The path beneath your feet turns into pavement and you realize you're running down a street—*your* street. Up ahead your house pops into view.

You're about to reach your door when the bunny halts and sits frozen, listening. Soon you hear it too—the snarling, yowling, and yipping of a pack of dogs.

"Run!" you cry.

"But I wanted to take you all the way home," he wails.

"I *am* home," you say.

"Not quite," replies the bunny as he races away. "You'll see."

See what? you wonder as you try to open the front door. It's still locked from the night before, so you decide to climb through your bedroom window.

Turn to page 53.

42 "You're *no* distance from home," says the bunny.

"How can you say that?" you ask impatiently. "You can see my house isn't here."

"It's not here," the bunny replies, "because you have not traveled in distance, but in *time*. We are still in your backyard, but we've gone back three hundred years, and your house wasn't here then."

On hearing that, you sit on the ground and try to think. The bunny hops on through the woods.

If you follow the bunny, turn to page 16.

If you decide to explore the woods on your own, turn to page 34.

There's something about this bunny that looks very familiar!

"May I hold it?" you ask.

"Sure."

You hold the bunny in your arms. Its fur is soft and its body quivering and warm. You close your eyes for a moment. When you open them, you're still holding the bunny, but now you're sitting with your own family in your own home and having breakfast on Easter morning!

"Are you feeling all right?" your mom asks.

"This is *some* bunny," you say.

The End

44   "I thought we were going into the future, but we're back in the Ice Age," you tell the bunny through chattering teeth.

"We *are* in the future—right where your house was—twenty-five thousand years ago!"

A blast of wind strikes you. You stand, shivering, feeling weak and numb.

"Come on," the bunny says.

You rub your freezing ears. "I can't go on. I'm too cold to move."

"You'd better hurry," the bunny says, hopping awkwardly through the snow.

If you force yourself to follow the bunny, turn to page 14.

If you flop down in the snow, turn to page 48.

46 The bunny is now running through the tall, damp grass. You struggle to keep up. You stumble and sprawl on the ground. It's suddenly cooler. The grass is in your own backyard!

As you sit up, you see the bunny watching as if to make sure you're all right. You're still a little scared and you run into the house, almost bumping into your mom.

"Happy Easter!" she says.

"Happy Easter, Mom!"

Your mom brushes some grass and mud off your jeans. "What were you doing outside so early?" she asks.

You wonder whether she'll believe your story: "I know what the Easter bunny knows—what was here before our house was built, and long before that, and long before that."

The End

48 You can't go on. You flop in the snow. You're beginning to feel numb. Maybe you'll wake up in a minute, maybe not. It doesn't matter, it's just too cold.

You're shivering terribly. Your hands feel clammy. You're so cold. If only you had more blankets. Blankets! You do have a blanket! You're in bed. Safe! Though you're certainly sick. You look around—there's your mom bringing a big quilt.

"I'm afraid you have a terrible chill," she says, feeling your forehead. "I'll take your temperature."

"Happy Easter, Mom!"

"Happy Easter," she says as she gives you a kiss. "You sound happy even though you're sick!"

"I am, Mom. Say, could you look in the backyard and see if there's a bunny out there?"

The End

50   As you start down the path to the left, you notice another strange thing. The trees here are bigger and farther apart. The forest floor is covered with pine needles and matted leaves. Then you see the bunny, farther along the path.

"I'm glad you came this way," the bunny says.

You feel a little silly talking to a rabbit, but you decide to ask a question anyway. "How far away am I from home?"

Turn to page 42.

As you push aside the curtain, you gasp. On your wall, where your Dwight Gooden poster should be, is a picture of Bert and Ernie. In the corner, where your bed should be, is a crib. And in the crib is a baby.

The baby turns over in its sleep, so you can see its face. It's the face you had as a baby. It's you!

You're wondering what to do when you hear laughing. It's the bunny, hopping toward you through the grass.

"What a pack of dummies," he says. "I shook 'em off my trail. Now I can get you all the way back to your own time."

He leaps into your arms and suddenly you're back in bed on Easter morning! Where did the baby go? you wonder. Then you smile, as you think back, remembering your very first Easter.

The End

ABOUT THE AUTHOR

Edward Packard is a graduate of Princeton University and Columbia Law School. He developed the unique storytelling approach used in the Choose Your Own Adventure® series while thinking up stories for his children, Caroline, Andrea, and Wells.

ABOUT THE ILLUSTRATOR

Vincent Bell is an award-winning artist, who has worked in animation for over thirty-three years. Mr. Bell has animated a number of theatrical shorts and more than five hundred of the top commercial spots in the television industry. The illustrator currently lives in Port Chester, New York.

CHOOSE YOUR OWN ADVENTURE

SKYLARK EDITIONS

☐	15480	The Green Slime #6 S. Saunders	$2.25
☐	15195	Help! You're Shrinking #7 E. Packard	$1.95
☐	15496	Indian Trail #8 R. A. Montgomery	$2.25
☐	15506	Dream Trips #9 E. Packard	$2.25
☐	15495	The Genie In the Bottle #10 J. Razzi	$2.25
☐	15222	The Big Foot Mystery #11 L. Sonberg	$1.95
☐	15424	The Creature From Miller's Pond #12 S. Saunders	$2.25
☐	15226	Jungle Safari #13 E. Packard	$1.95
☐	15442	The Search For Champ #14 S. Gilligan	$2.25
☐	15444	Three Wishes #15 S. Gilligan	$2.25
☐	15465	Dragons! #16 J. Razzi	$2.25
☐	15489	Wild Horse Country #17 L. Sonberg	$2.25
☐	15262	Summer Camp #18 J. Gitenstein	$1.95
☐	15490	The Tower of London #19 S. Saunders	$2.25
☐	15501	Trouble In Space #20 J. Woodcock	$2.25
☐	15283	Mona Is Missing #21 S. Gilligan	$1.95
☐	15418	The Evil Wizard #22 A. Packard	$2.25
☐	15305	The Flying Carpet #25 J. Razzi	$1.95
☐	15318	The Magic Path #26 J. Goodman	$1.95
☐	15467	Ice Cave #27 Saunders, Packard	$2.25
☐	15342	The Fairy Kidnap #29 S. Gilligan	$1.95
☐	25463	Runaway Spaceship #30 S. Saunders	$2.25
☐	15508	Lost Dog! #31 R. A. Montgomery	$2.25
☐	15379	Blizzard of Black Swan #32 Saunders/Packard	$2.25
☐	15380	Haunted Harbor #33 S. Gilligan	$2.25
☐	15399	Attack of the Monster Plants #34 S. Saunders	$2.25

Prices and availability subject to change without notice.